W9-BNN-048

For the Bear himself
V.P.

VIKING
Published by the Penguin Group
Penguin Putnam Books for Young Readers, 345 Hudson Street, New York, New York 10014, U.S.A.
Penguin Books Ltd, 27 Wrights Lane, London W8 5TZ, England
Penguin Books Australia Ltd, Ringwood, Victoria, Australia
Penguin Books Canada Ltd, 10 Alcorn Avenue, Toronto, Ontario, Canada M4V 3B2
Penguin Books (N.Z.) Ltd, 182-190 Wairau Road, Auckland 10, New Zealand

Penguin Books Ltd, Registered Offices: Harmondsworth, Middlesex, England

First published in Great Britain by Hodder Children's Books, a division of Hodder Headline Limited, 2001.
First published in the United States of America by Viking, a division of Penguin Putnam Books for Young Readers, 2002.

1 3 5 7 9 10 8 6 4 2

LIBRARY OF CONGRESS CATALOGING-IN-PUBLICATION DATA IS AVAILABLE.

ISBN 0-670-03546-7

Printed in Hong Kong
Set in Tiplex and Slappy

Bearum Scarum

written by
VIC PARKER

illustrated by
EMILY BOLAM

VIKING

Ten hairy hunters are out to find a bear.

Ten hairy hunters are searching everywhere.

Ten hairy hunters discover Bear's tracks . . .

Shhh! Bear's friends are right behind their backs.

Ten hairy hunters start following the trail.

Ten hairy hunters are hot on Bear's tail.

Ten hairy hunters head into the unknown.

Shhh! Bear's friends do some hunting of their own.

Nine hairy hunters at the edge of a ridge.

Nine hairy hunters see there isn't any bridge.

Nine hairy hunters swing across as best they can.

Shhh! Bear's friends take away another man.

Eight hairy hunters reach a muddy bog.

Eight hairy hunters inch across a log.

Eight hairy hunters wobble on their way.

Shhh! Bear's friends steal another man away.

Seven hairy hunters hit a cliff and stop.

Seven hairy hunters need to reach the top.

Seven hairy hunters climb toward the sun.

Shhh! Bear's friends have caught another one.

Six hairy hunters dig a deep, dark pit.

Six hairy hunters bring some leaves to cover it.

Six hairy hunters make a trap to catch a bear.

Shhh! Bear's friends have caught one in their snare.

Five hairy hunters have to take a little swim.

Five hairy hunters hold their breath and jump right in.

Five hairy hunters go splashing toward the shore.

Shhh! Bear's friends snap and take away one more.

Four hairy hunters take a tunnel through the trees.
Four hairy hunters crawling low on hands and knees.
Four hairy hunters squeeze along to reach the light.
Shhh! Bear's friends snatch another out of sight.

Three hairy hunters set some honey out for bait.

Three hairy hunters settle down to wait.

Three hairy hunters fall asleep and snore.

Shhh! Bear's friends have carried off one more.

Two hairy hunters go creeping up on Bear.

Two hairy hunters don't want Bear to see them there.

Two hairy hunters are sneaking very near.

Shhh! Bear's friends make one hunter disappear.

One hairy hunter comes face to face with Bear.

One hairy hunter thinks he's got Bear fair and square.

One hairy hunter looks deep into Bear's eyes.

One hairy hunter gets a very **big** surprise—
Arrgghhhh!

No hairy hunters left—they're all on the run.

No hairy hunters left—Bear's friends have won.

No hairy hunters left—Bear is happy, too.